Fergus
in the Park

Dedicated to
Cannon Hill Park, Birmingham,
where as a child I enjoyed
many happy family outings.

First published in 1998 in Great Britain by
Piccadilly Press Ltd, London
www.piccadillypress.co.uk

Text and illustrations copyright © Tony Maddox 1998

This 2010 edition published by Sandy Creek by arrangement with Piccadilly Press

Sandy Creek
122 Fifth Avenue
New York, NY 10011

ISBN: 978 1 4351 2327 4

1 3 5 7 9 10 8 6 4 2

Printed and bound in China

Fergus in the Park

Tony Maddox

Sandy Creek

Fergus was waiting in
the truck for Farmer Bob.
It was a warm, sunny day.

He could see the park across the street.
It looked cool and inviting.

He knew he should
stay in the truck, but the
park was too tempting.
He jumped down and
went to take a look.

"This is better than sitting in the back of Farmer Bob's old truck," he thought, as he strolled through the trees.

He stopped to watch the skateboarders zooming up and down.

He began to imagine that he was a champion skateboarder, performing all sorts of tricks. Wouldn't that be fun?

His daydreams were broken by
an angry shout behind him.

He turned to see a park worker
hurrying towards him.

"Can't you read?" he demanded,
pointing to a large sign.
Fergus was puzzled.
"What a silly question," he thought.
"Of course I can't read. I'm a dog!"

In this situation, the best thing to do was …

RUN!

Through the park he raced, with the park worker close behind. Other dogs, excited by all the commotion, broke loose from their owners and joined in the chase.

The park worker was getting closer and closer.
"He's going to catch me!" groaned Fergus.

When he saw a
skateboard lying at
the edge of the path,
he jumped on it,
and off he went!

People scattered as he whizzed along.

He was going *FASTER*…

and *FASTER*…

and *FASTER*.

The lake was just ahead…

Boats for HIRE

HOW WAS HE GOING TO STOP?

Too late! There he was…
flying UP…UP…UP into the air…
and then *down…down …down*

into the lake with a great *BIG SPLASH!*

He began to swim towards the
island in the middle of the lake.
"I'll be safe there," he gasped.

But he wasn't…
The park worker was
climbing into a row boat.
He was coming out to the island!
"This is turning into a really bad day!"
sighed Fergus, miserably.

But help was at hand.
The ducks who lived on the island
thought of a way Fergus could escape
without the park worker knowing.

Together, with Fergus hidden in the middle,
they paddled slowly past the park worker
and back to the park.

As Fergus hurried back to Farmer Bob's truck, the ducks kept the park worker busy by surrounding his boat, flapping their wings and making lots of noise.

"Sorry I've taken so long, Fergus,"
said Farmer Bob when he returned.

"I know! Since you've been so good,
we'll go for a walk in the park!"